TOUCAN WITH TWO CANS

By Heidi E. Y. Stemple

Illustrated by Aaron Spurgeon

Ready-to-Read

Simon Spotlight
New York   London   Toronto   Sydney   New Delhi

For Siobhan: Thank you for being
the first Toucan fan.
—H. E. Y. S.

Thank you, Lydia and Jackie Raye,
for being the best company in
quarantine a human can have.
—with love, Aaron

SIMON SPOTLIGHT

An imprint of Simon & Schuster Children's Publishing Division

1230 Avenue of the Americas, New York, New York 10020

This Simon Spotlight edition August 2021

Text copyright © 2021 by Heidi E. Y. Stemple

Illustrations copyright © 2021 by Aaron Spurgeon

For information about special discounts for bulk purchases, please contact

Simon & Schuster Special Sales at 1-866-506-1949 or business@simonandschuster.com.

Manufactured in the United States of America 0721 LAK

10 9 8 7 6 5 4 3 2 1

Library of Congress Cataloging-in-Publication Data

Names: Stemple, Heidi E. Y., author. | Spurgeon, Aaron, illustrator.

Title: Toucan with two cans / by Heidi E. Y. Stemple ; illustrated by Aaron Spurgeon.

Description: Simon Spotlight edition. | New York : Simon Spotlight, 2021. | Series: Ready-to-read

Audience: Ages 4–6. | Audience: Grades K-1. | Summary: "Can Toucan juggle two cans? He can! What about

three cans? Or four? Can you root for Toucan and his can juggling act?"— Provided by publisher.

Identifiers: LCCN 2021003349 (print) | LCCN 2021003350 (ebook)

ISBN 9781534485938 (hardcover) | ISBN 9781534485921 (paperback) | ISBN 9781534485945 (ebook)

Subjects: CYAC: Stories in rhyme. | Toucans—Fiction. | Juggling—Fiction.

Classification: LCC PZ8.3.S8228 To 2021 (print) | LCC PZ8.3.S8228 (ebook) | DDC [E]—dc23

LC record available at https://lccn.loc.gov/2021003349

LC ebook record available at https://lccn.loc.gov/2021003350

Two cans and Toucan.

I see how this can be fun!

Take your seats
so we can watch Toucan.

One can,
two cans.

Three cans?

Can he?

Can he, safely?

Toucans
can be fans
of Toucan with three cans.

It is hot!
The fan toucans
need one, two,
and three fans.

Who will fan Toucan
as he juggles all three cans?

The fans?

Enter the dancers
dancing the can-can

each with a fan
fanning juggling Toucan.

One can,

two cans,

three cans,

now four cans!

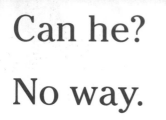

Can he?

No way.

No way?

Well, maybe . . .

Finally!
Toucan
juggles with FIVE cans!

Toucan's fans cheer
from up here
in the stands.

Hip, hip, hooray
for Toucan
and five cans!

Oh no!
One can,

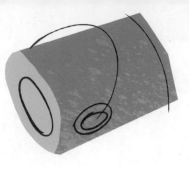

then two cans,

then three, four,
and five cans

land on the ground
with a loud *boom,*

bang,

ka-blam!

The fans
in the stands
fall silent. . . .

Then Toucan bows low,
and all his fans

know—

this is the end
of the Toucan can show.